Horses and Ponies

By Rosanna Hansen
Illustrated by Peter Barrett

For Rebecca and Emmalyn

A GOLDEN BOOK • NEW YORK
Western Publishing Company, Inc., Racine, Wisconsin 53404

E F G H I J K L M

Back in the days of your great-great grandparents, most children learned to ride a horse when they were very young. Their horses carried them to school or to market, or wherever they needed to go. There weren't any cars or trucks in those days, so horses were the most important helpers people had. Horses plowed the fields, pulled wagons, and carried people everywhere.

Today, we have cars and trains and airplanes, but horses are still important to us. Now, more than ever, people like to ride them for sport and for fun. There are over nine million horses in America today, and that number is growing steadily. Pleasure riding, racing, jumping, and horse shows are becoming more popular each year. For everyone who loves them, horses will always be a very special part of our world.

ALL ABOUT HORSES

A horse is built for speed. With its long legs and strong muscles it can run fast for miles at a time. Its feet end in hard hooves that protect it while it runs. The hooves are like very thick toenails. They can be cut, or horseshoes can be nailed to them, without hurting the horse.

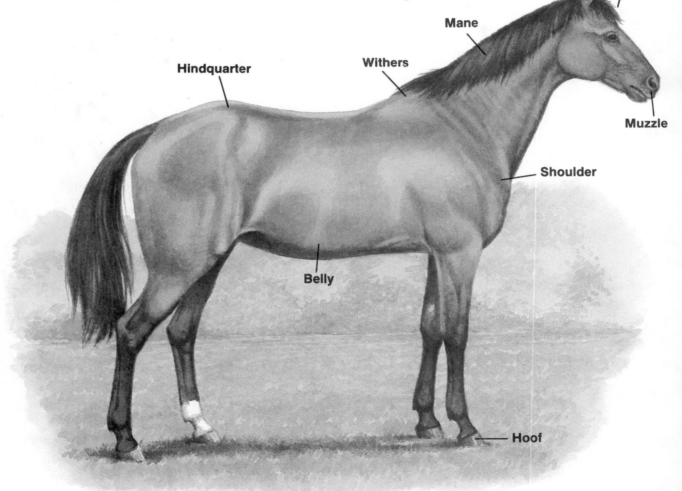

Forelock

Mane

Withers

Hindquarter

Muzzle

Shoulder

Belly

Hoof

    People measure how tall a horse is by putting their
hands next to one another from the ground up to the base
of the horse's neck, or withers. One hand is about 4
inches wide. So a horse that is 64 inches tall at the
withers would be 16 hands high.
    This picture shows a horse that is 60 inches tall at the
withers. If you count the hands, you will see that the
horse is 15 hands high.

At one time all the horses in the world were wild. Then, about 4,000 years ago, people began to tame the wild horses. As time passed they learned to use different kinds of horses for different jobs—carrying people, plowing fields, pulling loads, and more. They found that some horses were good at one kind of job, and some were good at other jobs.

Today, there are three main kinds of horses. You can tell them apart by their size, how they look, and what jobs they do.

Heavy Horses

Since they are big powerful animals with thick legs and strong muscles, heavy horses can pull large loads with ease. At shows they are judged on their strength and their pulling ability. These gentle giants sometimes weigh as much as 2,000 pounds—twice the weight of most light horses. They usually stand about 16 hands high.

There are several different types, or breeds, of heavy horses. The Shire, which is the largest, often stands more than 17 hands high and weighs over 2,000 pounds. Other breeds include the Clydesdale, the Belgian, and the Percheron.

Light Horses

Smaller, faster, and more graceful than their bigger cousins, light horses weigh from 900 to 1,400 pounds. They usually stand about 15 hands high. Light horses are used for pleasure riding and for many other jobs. They herd cattle, pull carriages, compete in horse shows, run races, and more.

There are many different breeds of light horses. The Arabian, the Thoroughbred, the Quarter Horse, and the Morgan are some of the most popular breeds.

Ponies

Some people think that ponies are young horses, but that isn't true. They are really special breeds of little horses and are the smallest members of the horse family. The most popular breeds of pony are the Shetland and the Welsh.

Ponies usually stand 10 to 12 hands high and never stand higher than 14.2 hands. They usually weigh between 500 and 900 pounds. Ponies have the special job of helping children learn to ride, and they are also used to pull light carriages.

A HORSE'S LIFE

When we talk about horses, we use different names for different times in their lives. At birth a baby horse is called a foal. It weighs about 100 pounds and has long skinny legs. A few minutes after it is born the foal tries to stand up. Soon it will wobble over to its mother and begin to nurse. By the time it is one day old the foal can run fast enough to keep up with its mother!

Foals stay close to their mothers and drink their milk until they are about six months old. By this time they are frisky little animals and love to run and play. From six months through age four the boy horses are called colts, and the girls are called fillies.

After their first birthday, both colts and fillies are called yearlings. Now they are old enough to start learning about saddles and riding.

By the time they are two years old the young horses have almost reached their full height. They have not finished growing, though. Their bones and muscles will not be fully grown until they are five. At that age the young horses become adults. The males are now called stallions, and the females are called mares.

THE ARABIAN

The Arabian is the oldest breed of horse in the world. More than a thousand years ago tribesmen in the deserts of Arabia were already breeding these beautiful horses. The tribesmen bred their horses for speed as well as toughness. The animals had to be tough to survive the long, hot trips through the desert.

The Arabian has several features that set it apart from other horses. Its neck is long and proudly arched. Its lean, noble-looking head tapers to a delicate muzzle. Although it is a small, stocky horse, it is strong for its size and likes to work hard.

Because of its beauty, intelligence, and friendliness, the Arabian is one of the best loved of all horses.

THE THOROUGHBRED

Champion of the racetrack—that's the Thoroughbred. For more than 200 years Thoroughbreds have been raised to be fine racehorses. The result is the fastest horses the world has ever known. At full speed a Thoroughbred can run as fast as 40 miles an hour for distances of up to 2 miles.

Every Thoroughbred alive today can trace its family back to one of three Arabian stallions that lived in the 1800's. When these stallions were bred with English mares, fine racehorses were the result.

The Thoroughbred is a large horse with a long body and a small head. It is easily excited and needs gentle, yet firm handling. Each year millions of people go to the racetrack for the thrill of watching the handsome Thoroughbreds compete.

THE QUARTER HORSE

The Quarter Horse is the most famous American breed in the world. This hard-working horse herds cattle throughout the American West and in many other countries, and it is popular for pleasure riding, too. Its name comes from its speed in running short distances. The Quarter Horse can run a quarter-mile faster than any other breed, and that is how it got its name.

Short legs and powerful hindquarters help the Quarter Horse get a quick start, turn quickly, and run fast. The Quarter Horse is also known for its calm manner and its ability to work hard.

THE MORGAN

The Morgan can trace its history back to a famous stallion known as Justin Morgan. This small handsome stallion could outpull and outrace most other horses of its day. Today, Morgan horses are known for the same things that made Justin Morgan famous. Their energy, strength, good looks, and gentleness have made them popular as riding horses throughout America.

THE AMERICAN SADDLEBRED

The American Saddlebred is the handsome, high-stepping star of the show ring. Its liveliness and good looks make it fun to watch or to ride. This spirited horse often learns five gaits, or ways of moving. Most horses know three normal gaits—the walk, the trot, and the gallop.

Because of its lively style in the show ring, the Saddlebred is often called the peacock of the horse world.

COLOR BREEDS

Some colorful types of horses are classed in special color breeds. The golden Palomino and the spotted Appaloosa are two of these color breeds.

The Palomino All Palominos have a golden coat with a white mane and tail. Sometimes they also have white markings on their face and below their knees. Because of their beautiful color, Palominos are often seen in circuses, parades, and movies.

The Appaloosa For hundreds of years the Nez Percé Indians of the Northwest raised a special kind of spotted horse. These Indian horses were sure-footed and fast, and they always had a spotted coat.

The Nez Percé Indians lived near the Palouse River in Idaho, and this river gave the spotted horse its name. At first, people called it "a Palouse" horse. After many years, the name became "Appaloosa." Today, the Appaloosa is used on ranches as a cow pony and is also a popular riding horse.

THE TENNESSEE WALKING HORSE

These handsome horses were developed by southern plantation owners in the 1880's. The plantation owners wanted a horse with a comfortable ride for traveling around their large farms. The easy-stepping Tennessee Walking Horse was the answer.

Today, Tennessee Walkers are known for their smooth "running walk" and easy canter. Some people say that riding a Tennessee Walker feels just like sitting in an old-fashioned rocking chair.

THE SHETLAND PONY

The shaggy little Shetland is the most famous pony in the world. It is also the smallest pony, standing only 9 to 11 hands high.

Shetlands have short, stocky bodies with a full mane and tail. In the winter their coats grow long and shaggy to keep them warm. Because of their size, Shetland ponies are a favorite mount for young children.

THE WELSH PONY

The Welsh pony is much larger than the Shetland. It stands about 12 hands high and weighs around 500 pounds. Because of its size, the Welsh pony is popular with children who have outgrown the Shetland but are too small for a full-size horse.

Welsh ponies are prized for their good looks and gentle nature. Their beauty comes in part from the Arabian blood in their veins. Over a hundred years ago an Arabian stallion was bred with some Welsh mares. Since then, the fine lines of the Arabian can be seen in Welsh ponies.

If you love horses and want to learn to ride well, you have picked a good hobby. Horses and riding can bring you pleasure for many, many years. When you care for a horse and learn to ride it, you can become its special friend.

There is no thrill in the world like a fast gallop, with you and your horse moving perfectly together as the countryside flashes by. And there is no friend in the world quite like the friend a horse can be.